# Bad Bye, Good Bye

Written by **Deborah Underwood**    Illustrated by **Jonathan Bean**

**HOUGHTON MIFFLIN HARCOURT**
Boston  New York

For Peggy
— D.U.

For Steve and Cherie
—J.B.

www.hmhbooks.com

The text of this book is set in Serifa Std.
The illustrations are ink and Prismacolor tone.

Library of Congress Cataloging-in-Publication Data
Underwood, Deborah.
Bad bye, good bye / written by Deborah Underwood ; illustrated by Jonathan Bean.
pp.  cm.
Summary: Illustrations and simple, rhyming text follow a family as they move to a new town.
ISBN 978-0-547-92852-4
[1. Stories in rhyme. 2. Moving, Household—Fiction.]  I. Bean, Jonathan, 1979– illustrator. II. Title.
PZ8.3.U562Bad 2014
[E]—dc23
2013017616

Manufactured in China
SCP 10 9 8 7 6 5 4 3 2 1
4500451627

Bad day
Bad box

Bad mop

Bad blocks

Bad truck

Bad guy

Bad wave

Bad bye

Stuffed car

Hot seat

Gray clouds

Gold wheat

Nice dog
Huge map

Smooth glass
Long nap

Truck horn

Pink dice

Blue pool

Loud ice

Big hair
White deer

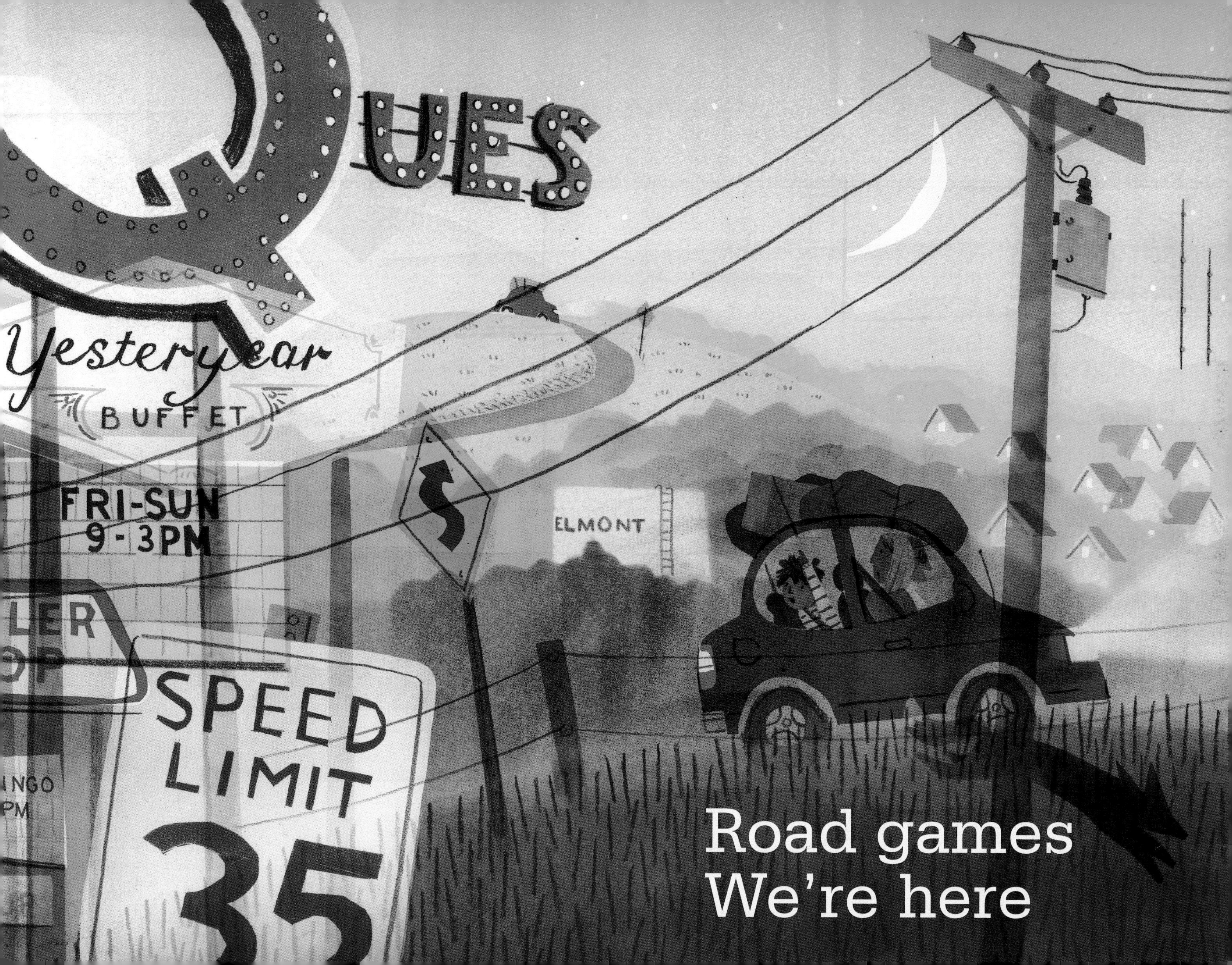


Road games
We're here

New town

New park

New street
New bark

New house
New hall

New room
New wall

New kid

Good throw

New bugs

Good glow

Good tree

Good sky

Good friend

Good bye